MW01227452

The Pulse between Dimensions and the Desert

"Rios de la Luz's writing blows minds and breaks hearts. A sort of new and bizarre Tomás Rivera, Rios is able to blend the familiar of the domestic with the all the wilderness of the universe. Her stories will grab you in places you didn't know you had, take you by those places to where you've always wanted to go—though you never knew how to get there. Buy this book and enjoy that journey." —Brian Allen Carr

"In *The Pulse between Dimensions and the Desert,* Rios de la Luz's writing is electric and alive. It grabs you and pulls you into her universe, one that is both familiar and foreign, a place where Martians find love, bad guys get their ears cut off, and time travel agents save lost children. In this innovative, heartfelt debut, de la Luz takes her place as a young author that demands to be read and watched." —Juliet Escoria

L a d y b o x .

♥

A Ladybox collection

Ladybox Books
10765 SW Murdock Lane
Apt. G6
Tigard, OR 97224

Cover art and design copyright © 2014 by Matthew Revert
www.matthewrevert.com

Interior design by J David Osborne

ISBN: 978-1-940885-18-6

Printed in the USA.

THE PULSE

BETWEEN

DIMENSIONS

AND THE DESERT

RIOS DE LA LUZ

LADYBOX BOOKS
PORTLAND, OR

For my sisters y las mujeres in my family.

TABLE OF CONTENTS

Martian Matters	1
Lupe and her Time Machine	5
Crayons	15
Hammer	19
Ear to the Ground	25
Morena	33
Curls	35
Enojada	37
Tarot	39
Colorado	41
The Pulse between Dimensions and the Desert	45
Church Bush	55
La Loba	61
Lady Mescaline	63
Esmai	65
Rosario	79
Las Mujeres	83
Sweet Gum	89
La Reina	95
Marigolds	99

MARTIAN MATTERS

Saturday means a call from your abuela. She asks you if you have a boyfriend. It is a guaranteed question. Every single time. "Grandma, no tengo un boyfriend." She insists that having a boyfriend means stability and better self-esteem. No man has ever put a hand on you because it sounds uncomfortable. You kissed a boy once, but the chemistry was forced and his excitement made you gag. He asked if you were okay then tried to kiss you again. You shoved him away and jumped out of his blue Sentra. He was embarrassed, so he spread rumors about you being queer. This was high school, right. He used the term queer with negative connotations. You use queer as an exclamation of who you are. Abuela doesn't know. You might say something to her about it after she's disintegrated into dust and can't tell you that looking for a girlfriend is ludicrous. "Mija, what show are you watching right now?" You slept for twelve hours after binge-watching an historical drama about ghosts and black magic. You can at least tell her about your Korean telenovelas with enthusiasm.

* * *

You wake up from a dream and you think it's real, right? You meet your soul mate in a planetarium on Mars. She's a Martian, you're a human prototype, but you go down on each other anyway, beneath the cosmic replicas in the tiny fortress that overlooks the pale blue dot called earth and the real stars birthing themselves and exploding into nothingness. You wake up and she doesn't exist. You do, but you're not really sure why. In other dreams, there is a lot of dark space. Shadows overtake the corners of your vision. There are three orenji koi fish that swim in the gray skies as you run through lush green fields looking for the Martian. She's a continuous theme after you've fallen asleep. The continuity you experience in three dimensions is nine to five. In the next dream you're hauling your TV onto a cliff and into the ocean. The three koi burst out of the sea and one swallows the TV. Its belly is bloated and it flickers on and off with flashes of a woman who is staring through to you. You wake up and realize you would never give up your TV.

Abuela says she will watch your Korean dramas when they are all subbed in Spanish. "Mija, are you looking for another job?" You used to work two jobs. Retail and banking. You were enthusiastic about the prospect of paying loans off early and traveling around by thirty-five. You quit retail on an impulse. A woman with puffy blonde hair yelled at you about a misplaced sign and singled you out by claiming the "ethnics" were messing up the country. You read an Urrea quote online that you wanted to say, but didn't. You wanted to say, "Listen puta, my ancestors may have crossed a river to get here, but your ancestors crossed oceans to be here and you think we owe you colonizers something? FUCK YOU." Instead, you took your apron off, threw it on the floor and ugly cried while she insisted on speaking to your manager.

When you fell asleep, dreams trapped you in that god damned mall. You drowned the first night. The second night, you kicked the shit out of giant crickets in the food court. The third night, the mall melted around you and sank into a volcano as you watched the fish fly over you in the pink sky. Your TV was still in the belly of the chubbiest koi. The Martian came back. She waved and smiled within the television screen as the fish flew toward the coast.

You tell abuela that one job is sustaining you for now. The bank job is exhausting. You don't speak Spanish as well as you used to, but you can help some of tu gente when they come in. The relief on the faces of the women you interact with gives you warmth. You can help them for a brief moment and they can remain strangers to you. You don't know many people in this city. You've been staying alone in your apartment the past six months. You moved away so you wouldn't have to answer your door in the town you grew up in. The chances of running into cruel assholes were high. In the town you used to live, you chose comic books over people. You chose music over people. You chose dreaming over people.

* * *

The Martian showed up in the background of a dream when you first moved to Oregon. She was taking a photo with a faceless person. She had her peace sign up and the camera flashed multiple times until you were transported into a space vessel. You had a phaser on hand as you rode up an elevator with blinking buttons on the ceiling and next to the doors. You snuck out of the elevator and space soldiers in ninja gear chased after you with laser guns.

The Martian remained frequent in your head. She isn't real, and you understand this thoroughly. She isn't real and you understand this with a heavy heart.

"Mija, when are you going to visit me?" You say "soon." Abuela tells you she loves you and this is a fact. You can rely on her for that. Your body hurts. It all stems from your feet. You start a bath with no bubbles. You tell abuela to have a good night and that you'll talk to her next Saturday.

The Martian wakes up in the core of her planet. She is born out of stardust like everything else. Her first dream is about a world of faceless creatures and three koi flying past her toward a pale blue dot in the black sky.

LUPE
AND HER TIME MACHINE

The winter wind took Guadalupe's breath away. This was the year it snowed on Christmas Eve in El Paso. She stepped out early in the morning, thinking about the bus route to the mercado. Crouched over, she regained her vitality. She hit her chest with her small fist and coughed out a curse. The cold was unforgiving. Lupe shivered and blew hot air into her shaking hands. Her supermarket visit was short. She stepped back onto the bus en route to her place. When the bus dropped her off on the corner of Figueroa and Pelicanos, she stomped into her turquoise casa. She dropped her paper bag full of produce and ran toward the round mirror in the hallway. The mirror showed her the seasonal cracks in her hands and lips. The dried blood in between crevices of senescent skin. The winter reminded Lupe of her inevitable biological disposition. Her position as abuela growing longer and longer with time. Focusing into the mirror, she saw dehydrated flakes of skin latching onto wrinkles in their final moments. She saw silver strands of hair overtaking her head. Lupe brushed through the peppered follicles and said her age aloud. She said her age aloud once more and thought about the day her grandchildren would bury her. Their faces burning from the loss, but their minds prepared to continue living. She shuddered. This was Guadalupe's reason for praying on behalf of her family in the mornings. She lights all the candles in the house and pours a cup of coffee, then she whispers into the atmosphere and watches the candles wither into stumps.

Sometimes, Lupe burns from chile on her tongue, other times the burning comes from witnessing what her child Alma is going through because of an hombre with an ego deeper than the darkest blues of the ocean. They have found the strangest creatures down there and this man is no exception. He drowns in his machismo. He is strange to Lupe because he claims to love Alma, but he hits her. He leaves her marked up and brings her to Lupe's house with no regard for what he does. Lupe cringes when he grabs Alma by the waist or interlocks his hands into hers. Every connected finger signaling a silent apology. Last year, Alma learned how to drive at Lupe's pleading. If Alma learned how to drive, she could potentially drive away from that situation. This is what Lupe prayed for. Lupe has kept her opinions of the hombre to herself. The men Lupe loved withered physically and passed on or disappeared after a child started developing in her womb. She felt she had no room to speak.

Lupe has four grandchildren from Alma. Fernando. Sandra. Benjamin. Noah. They are loud and expressive with their emotions. They are not afraid to cry or laugh. Their eyes show curiosity. Lupe sees this as a milagro.

Their father is quiet and has never warmed up to her. He does not smile at her. He does not ask Lupe how her day was. He smokes and the scent lingers. Lupe has accumulated several migraines because of that hombre. He sits in spaces where he can be alone, usually outside or in the garage, but he's not allowed in the garage anymore. Lupe told Alma that he has to keep out. She even threw her shoe at him one day when he tried to go there without permission. Lupe is working on something big. She cannot share it with her family, but Dios knows what she's up to.

She whispers her prayer for the time machine before she starts working on it again. A pink bicycle helmet hides a French braid and electrician's gloves guard her hands. Lupe chose to wear her favorite black dress with red and purple flowers embroidered to embrace her shoulders and chest. She chose a purple jacket to match. She bought the dress as a celebration of raising children who loved her and children who called her every day. Her time machine is an oval device that is one foot taller than she is and wide enough to fit a family of five. The bottom of the machine is flat. Lupe installed checkered tile into the floor embossed with the faces of saints. Santa Rosa. La Virgen. Santa Catarina scattered in between black and white. Lupe washes her feet before she steps inside. The front of the machine has a standard control center with a big red START button. Lupe was instructed to hang multi-colored LED lights around the dashboard. She created stained glass sculptures and hung them with vines. Sugar skulls are stacked in an interior shelf of the machine. Lupe placed them there for her mother, father, abuela and her brother Jose. There are empty shelves that Lupe is planning on filling with books she found in bargain bins. They announced themselves to her. ASTRONOMY. QUANTAM PHYSICS. THE MILKY WAY GALAXY. The outer shell of the time machine has embroidered geometric patterns of reds, turquoise and violets. She is almost done filling the entire outer layer of the egg with color. She wants the top of the egg to have an embroidered sun and the bottom, a crescent moon.

The science behind the machine came in a dream. She woke up to find formulas and photographs tacked into her wall. The photos clarified the formulas and sometimes, they even gave her the bus routes to take for supplies. It took the entire summer. A couple new moons into fall, Lupe finally figured out that she was making a time machine. Building the machine became fun. She attached tree roots and electrical wires together. She hung vines in the grid ceiling of the egg. The vines carefully looping in and out of the open squares and making their way down the sides of the machine. Lupe stuck photos of her Chihuahua Cuca inside and another photo of her and the kids. Alma was still in diapers. Blanca and Elena wore matching floral dresses. Angie held onto her gold pendant of a rose hanging from a yellow string. Lupe never smiled in photos, but she was happy.

Lupe prayed before bed. She prayed for her grandchildren and then for her daughters. She prayed for Cuca and then for the machine. Sitting in bed, Lupe felt numbness overcome her body. She woke up to the shadow of a tall red faun looming over her. It whispered into her ear. This would be the final lesson. The time machine will only work under Lupe's command. She cannot pick where the time machine takes her. Lupe cannot stay within a chosen timeframe. She must come back. The red faun disappeared into a burst of gold glitter. Lupe braced herself and laughed into the empty space in her room.

Lupe stored forty-two pots and pans in the garage. She filled them to the brim with rose petals. They served as fuel for the machine. She grabbed a pot and dumped clumps of rose petals into the fuel opening. She stuck a cloth patch of a red rose on the START button. One button to shift her from a normal woman to a mad scientist. Lupe packed a small bag with a change of summer clothes, in case she went somewhere warm. She prayed. She pushed the button. She felt dizzy. She heard her kids. They were screaming excitedly at each other about the paletero. She heard her kids. They were calling out to her. Angie had a nightmare and told the other three. Now, they can't sleep.

Lupe walks into their room. This was the room with the planets aligned above the bed frame. Lupe painted those planets one Sunday instead of going to church. She picks Angie up and takes her to her room. She picks up baby Alma next, then Blanca, then Elena. She carries them all into her room. This was the room with different colored walls. Pink for Alma. Purple for Elena. Pastel yellow for Angie and sky blue for Blanca. Lupe tucks herself into bed and tells the kids about the time she got lost at the swap meet. The swap meet was a weekend tradition for Lupe and her mom.

Lupe wanted to look at the bins of beads on sale. She picked up each kind of bead, one by one, and carefully examined the itty bitty spheres as though they were worlds. She squinted at the beings on a silver planet and the bead flew out from in between her thumb and pointer finger. Lupe gasped and then got on her hands and knees to search for it. She can't remember how long it took to find the silver orb, but she found it eventually. After finding the bead she realized her mother was no longer behind her. She was lost. She panicked and ran down the aisle screaming MAMI MAMI. She even lost a chancla along the way.

Mis amores, I was so scared. I thought your grandma disappeared. Lloré y lloré. I cried until I reminded myself that your abuela was probably searching for me too. Me calmé. I asked some grown-ups if they saw a pretty woman with long red hair and a black dress on. A lot of the men said yes, and I followed their pointed fingers in the direction of tu abuela. When we found each other, she didn't curse me. She embraced me. I will always remember that moment with tu abuela. If you four are ever scared, let me know. Let me know and I will embrace you. I will carry you in my arms until you fall asleep.

Lupe sat still in her time machine. Her hands trembled in pace with the acceleration of her heart. She pushed the cloth rose again. She heard Vicente Fernandez echoing in the background. She heard a car screech as it struggled to start.

* * *

Lupe is standing in front of an hombre she once loved. He is living downtown with another woman. Lupe needs funds for Alma and the kids that aren't his. She wants to provide them with more. The kids grow and grow and Lupe can't keep up. Lupe is in a white tank top with a black bra on and a red skirt that flows against her body in the desert wind. She has a gold necklace on with pendants representing her four girls. She puffs out her chest and holds Alma on her hip. The other three are in the minivan. She demands compensation for the baby. She slams her fist against his front door and tells him to come out and face her. The coward cracks the door and tells her to get the fuck out of his vida. The coward walks outside, sticks his chest out como un pajaro, and calls the child illegitimate. Alma doesn't belong to anyone. He shouts these words into Lupe's ear. He shoves her. He keeps shoving her until she's on the ground. Alma is screaming. Lupe sits herself up, cradles Alma, kisses her forehead, looks up at the coward and tells him that she will see him in hell.

Lupe wanted to get out of the machine. She wanted to punch the coward in the jaw. Even if she broke her wrists, it would be worth it. She pushed down on the cloth rose again. She heard dance music playing at her brother's wedding. She heard *Sabado Gigante* blaring from a TV.

* * *

She hears Angie and Blanca fighting. Angie calls Blanca's skin ugly. Angie spits at Blanca and shouts at her to stay out of the fucking sun. Lupe grabs Angie by the hair and slaps her in the face. Don't you dare say that shit to your hermana. ¿Me entiendes? Angie shouts that hitting her won't deter her from telling Blanca how it is. She chases after Blanca. They go down in fists. Lupe struggles to pull them apart from each other. Little Elena and Alma press their bodies against the door where Angie is now locked inside. Lupe prays frantically as she sits in the machine. She stumbles out of the machine and her past freezes. She opens the door to get to Angie and she hugs her. She steps back out and holds onto each one of the girls and asks them to forgive each other.

Back inside the machine, Lupe slams her palms against the rose patch. She doesn't want to time travel anymore. She wants to see her grandchildren. She wants to tell them silly stories and make them paletas in ice cube trays with toothpicks and horchata. She lands in her garage. She shuts the door to the egg and crawls into her house. Lupe crawls into her living room and clutches her phone so hard, she thinks she hears it crack. She calls Alma and tells her to bring the kids and leave the quiet man at home. Alma hesitates over the phone, but 30 minutes later, she rings the doorbell with the four kids lined up behind her.

Lupe makes hot chocolate for the kids. All of the candles are lit. The kids sit in the living room and watch TV. Lupe runs into her room to gather more pillar candles. She places them throughout her shelves and on the tables. She lights them and asks Alma to help her grab some more. Alma gathers candles and tells Lupe to stop being weird. Lupe tells Alma she is sorry. Tell me if you are afraid. Let me know if you are scared. I will pray that you tell me. Lupe hugs Alma and expects a limp reaction. Alma hugs Lupe back and Lupe's sleeve becomes a dark pool of her daughter's tears. Alma is so silent, it frightens Lupe. Alma cleans her face with the bottom of her shirt and goes back into the living room to sit with the kids. They sit together and laugh at cartoons. The kids start to drift into sleep. Lupe helps Alma carry the kids into the van. She ensures they are secured properly by their seat belts and tells them one by one that she loves them. They leave and Lupe keeps the candles lit. She walks into the garage and opens the door to her machine again. She washes her feet. She steps into the colorful egg. She sits in the middle of the machine and falls asleep. In the morning, she decides to time travel again.

CRAYONS

During recess, I lugged the classroom's bucket of crayons, color pencils, and markers with me. The class played kickball and I sat under the shade of a palo verde tree because of asthma. I arranged all the greens together, blues together and reds together. I continued until they were all in front of me in their chromatic families. Red represented anger. Pink meant passion. Blue mirrored the bodies of water on the planet. Greens expressed curiosity. Yellows owned the sun. Naranjas represented astronauts with Martian dust on their boots. Brown was my favorite. Brown represented the people I interacted with every single day. My grandma, my little sister, all the people gathered downtown waiting for the bus. In a floppy notepad, I wrote the name of every color down. I signed for them all and then I became the principal. I checked in on the classes. Were the blues perfecting the science of creating drinking water from cumulonimbus clouds? Were the pinks writing poetry? I checked in on them all and wrote down their progress. I took the green marker and drew little vines on the white bench behind me and then on my left hand and up my arm. Recess was over. I dumped all the colors back into the bucket.

I shoved the bucket underneath the crafting area. I went to my desk and saw a pamphlet on my desk. The same pamphlet was placed on each desk in the class. The school wanted us to sell cookie dough. Mrs. Rodriguez asked us to participate and told us to open our pamphlets. Inside, I scanned the potential prizes. There were sticker sets and water guns, but an art case clutched onto my heart. The art case was pristine. Enclosed within was a rainbow organization of markers, color pencils, crayons, and sharpeners all neatly established in assigned creases. This suitcase of colors could be mine.

When I got home, I crawled on the floor of the single unit scavenging for a pencil. My scabbed knees slid across the cement floor that collected dust easily and caused my coughing fits each morning. I reached under the bed and found a standard no 2. In the bathroom, there was no tub, only a shower. I crawled into the cemented space underneath the toilet and thought about neighbors who might theoretically buy from me. There was the Cubana next door, with her high heels and hair as bright as when you look into the sun. She was not home often. Like my mamá, she worked a lot. When they went dancing together, mamá would wear her black dress with the circular cutouts on both sides of her hips and the Cubana wore lipstick deeper than a bloodline. The Cubana called me 'hermosa' and I called her 'muy amable' because I thought it was rude to ask an adult for their first name.

I was never asked to sell anything before. Mrs. Rodriguez explained how the accumulated profits would help in funding the school, but I was enthralled by the art set. I tore paper from a notebook and taped six pieces against the front door. I took out an extra order form from my backpack and cut out the picture of the art case. I taped it to the center of my makeshift billboard. I drew a line graph, a bar graph and a pie chart on the display. I drew arrows in black crayon that pointed to the art case and stars in yellow crayon to signify stellar importance. I went to each door in our row of living units. I knocked and asked for adults to buy from me. Most of them didn't answer. One woman answered and then asked me how a bucket of cookie dough would bring nutritional value to her bebé? I shrugged. I asked my sister if I could use her name to buy buckets of cookie dough. I pointed to the art set and explained that I needed to gain enough points for the prize and she nodded. I asked her what type of cookie dough she wanted. She nodded. I asked her if she wanted chocolate chip and peanut butter. She enthusiastically shook her head at me. I wrote her name out on each line and carefully calculated the amount of points needed to get the art set. I took her hand and helped her squiggle letters onto the signature lines with a pencil. I was so proud of my sister for understanding how this would benefit the both of us. Our eight piece set of crayons never detailed the true richness of blue in the desert sky or the brown depth in our hair.

Before class started, I turned in my order form to the office and the receptionist squinted at me, shook her head and said nothing. That morning, I brushed through my curly hair and it expanded beyond the padded shoulders of my passed-down sweatshirt. I smiled at myself as I brushed and brushed in front of the mirror. A girl in class told me my hair looked cuckoo ca choo. She asked me who did my hair and I told her it was my mamá. Recess started and I sat on the white bench under the palo verde tree. I traced the vines I drew on the bench the day before with my finger and watched the kids playing dodge ball. I didn't take the coloring bucket outside with me. Recess finished and I sat quietly at my desk until school was over for the day. I picked up my sister from my grandma's apartment on Alameda and we walked past fading billboard signs until we got to the empty unit. I locked us inside and cut up an apple for us to share. I pierced through my finger and watched the blood trickle into the dust beneath my bare feet. I told my sister that a bad guy cut my hand on my way to school and took my order forms. He didn't want cookie dough, but he wanted that art set so, we wouldn't be getting either prize anytime soon.

HAMMER

The line of twenty-four kids ahead of you shrinks as each person grabs an index card and obediently goes back to their seat. Your last name starts with a Z. You have adjusted to being last in alphabetical formations. The last card is waiting for you. Mrs. Espen announces the animal assigned and each one of you has been given the responsibility of deciding what to name it right then and there. You are all responsible for a storybook based on the assigned animal. Amanda Rosalia with the pink glasses and light up shoes names her Zebra "Ziggy." Jaime Santos with the bowl cut and dinosaur shirt names his bear "Brownie". The names continue to be announced and your palms are sweating. You link them together, open them toward you and look at the lifeline abuela told you about. You will live a healthy, productive life con el favor de Dios.

The next name is "Storm" for the stingray. "Mango" for the lion cub. "Henry" for the koala. You're up next and the index card has a strange sea creature on it. You ask Mrs. Espen if it's a mermaid. She smiles, braces covering her teeth, and says no. It's a hammerhead shark. What do you want to name your hammerhead shark? Startled by the new animal shifting your perception on wildlife and evolution, you blurt out "Hammer!" Hammer the hammerhead shark by Jocelyn Zavala. Mrs. Espen has made the official announcement and you can't take it back. Hammer will have to live with this label for the rest of her life so long as she exists in this story you make for her. Maybe she is one of those sharks who has been in trouble for her temper so "Hammer" stuck as a nickname. You don't know yet. You have to go home and discuss with Abuela and Mamá.

Mamá is cooking fideo because she's tired after a long day of moving pet food and merchandise around in her department. You help your brother and sister with their limes and then you squeeze half a lime into your bowl and warm your hands with the steam rising between the tomato sauce and noodles. Mamá tells Abuela about your cousin Stefani, who just turned ten. She is going to a private school and learning how to play guitar. She lives in Cali and auditions for commercials on the weekends. She's the cousin who you saw on TV when the apartment had cable for a month. She disappeared from the screen after the cable did so, you watched *Dragon Ball Z* en español on channel 2 in between TV fuzz and Univision.

Stefani was Goku and you were Piccolo. She had resources to be more powerful than you, but you never doubted your own strength. Stefani represented good and you shifted from evil to virtuous depending on the episode. You thought of yourself as evil when you acted on aggressions that came to you at night. You broke the limbs off of dolls and repaired them with duct tape in the morning. You drew on the faces of your sleeping siblings with eyeliner and then helped them wash it off in the morning. Once, you wrote "shit" as "chet" on your little sister's belly and told her to run up to mamá. Mamá was on the phone and yelled your full name (Jocelyn Esmeralda Mendoza Zavala) to help your sister get dressed for bed.

You finish your soup and ask Mamá and Abuela about story ideas for Hammer. Abuela suggests a story about Hammer being the Jesus of the sea. Hammer is the son of a carpenter and was born to a virgin mother shark. You tell Abuela that Hammer is a lady shark. You place your palms on your forehead and look at Mamá. Mamá suggests a story about Hammer as a shark who loses her memory. She is in the middle of the street under the sea, when she collapses and doesn't remember who she is anymore. Hammer was supposed to marry an heir to a company that specializes in wedding dresses. You grab your notebook and pencil out of your dandelion yellow backpack and crack your knuckles. You scribble: *Hammer, I am going to make you see the sea in yourself.* You write and erase. You write and keep erasing.

The next morning, the classroom is full of carried voices and foot taps to the linoleum squares beneath small feet. The teacher makes her way toward the chalkboard and announces new vocabulary words that will make you sound like a college kid. This is how she pulls you in. The first word is "grotesque". *Grotesque.* The second word is "idiosyncrasy". *Idiosyncrasy.* You repeat the words after her so they can stick to your tongue. Try using these words today. Energize your vocabulary, she says. Next, she asks the class to get into a single file line and place their math homework on her desk. She collects the stack and puts it into her rolling backpack. She reminds the class about the story book assignment. She expects it on her desk tomorrow morning. The index card with Hammer's picture is under your pillow. You thought Hammer would appear to you if you placed her beneath your sleepy head.

You search the library to look for more information on Hammer and come across articles of humans catching her relatives and displaying them like prizes. Humans attempted to tame Hammer's kin even though she represents protection, with her strange head and white belly. On your walk home from the library, a pink arch labeled "Dulcería" catches your eye. You walk underneath and find yourself at a carnival. The building is painted in pink and white vertical stripes. "La Vida es un Carnaval" is playing out of a boom box sitting on the dirt with a bouquet of balloons attached to the handle. No one is there, but you hear laughter. There are carnival games behind glass windows. You press your forehead against the glass where rubber ducks float in a blue pool. You knock on the window in case someone is behind there. You look to your feet and see green arrows. They lead you past the window displays and into a room with a claw machine. The machine is filled with stuffed animals of sea creatures. Jellyfish and squid are stacked with starfish and sharks. You grab the joystick and aim for the sharks. It takes you three tries before the claw gets a grasp of anything. Finally, you win the hammerhead shark. You throw your arms in the air and jump around. You start dancing with Celia Cruz singing "Contrapunto Musical." Confetti falls from above and the pieces that land on your tongue taste sweet.

When you get home, Mamá is making enchiladas verdes and she asks how your story is coming along. I figured it out in the Dulcería carnaval. Hammer reincarnated into a stuffed animal so I could meet her. Mamá laughs and asks you to get your brother and sister from the room upstairs. You go upstairs and see your sister sleeping on your pillow. You wonder if Hammer's past self is in her dream, taking her on an underwater quest. You write about the carnival. You write about Hammer's reincarnation. You decide to write more and more. Maybe a buddy cop movie with Hammer and a blue whale. Maybe hammer decides to go into space. You write these stories and read them to your brother and sister before bed. You write about Hammer every single day until you run out of ideas and have to focus on writing about yourself.

EAR TO THE GROUND

Soledad handed you a knife for Navidad. Let me show you how to use it, she said. She placed an apple on your head and told you to stand against the kitchen wall. She held onto the knife and shut one eye as she looked above you at the manzana. She threw the knife and it made a woosh sound into the bag of beans next to you. She praised you for not showing fear. She dug the knife out of the beans. You don't have to learn how to use the knife, but it could be beneficial. She patted your head and you smiled at her. When the knife was back in your hands, you hid it under your pillow and ran into the living room to sit next to Soledad. You watched stop motion movies together. The images birthed butterflies in your belly because you thought you were watching someone else's memory. You said this to Soledad and she told you she felt the same way. You both had Christmas sweaters on because Madre thought it was cute. You covered in penguins. Soledad covered in candy canes. You both ran for your matching red and green beanies and darted out of the house. You played tag around the pecan tree that marked the middle of the neighborhood. Soledad joked about magic powers in the tree.

"It talks to you if you put your ear to the ground."

She crouched toward the dirt then, she placed the side of her face toward the earth. She slapped her knee and laughed. You tapped your feet on the ground with impatience and fear of tree roots grabbing them. Soledad sat with criss-cross legs and reached up at you. You helped her up and watched the tree branches stretching themselves out toward the moonlight. Soledad hugged the trunk of the tree. Once boredom hit, the two of you ran back inside and drank warm horchata from mugs shaped like lizards and played lotería while Madre cooked pozole verde.

In the summer, you sliced open the stuffed jalapeño toys your madre sold to the people waiting in cars to get back to the U.S. You sewed them back up by hand and never told your mamá about the notes you placed inside them. "Be cool, stay in school." "Chill out, don't shout." "Hasta la vista, mamacita." The jalapeño pepper wore sunglasses and had a huge grin with little arms that gave the buyer a thumbs up. Como, it was saying, thank you for taking me away from this border town. You helped madre a couple times a week with newspaper and a spray bottle filled with watered down Windex. She told you to run up to the car and don't give them a choice, you spray the front window, take your newspaper and wipe that shit down before they can shoo you away. Look for U.S. license plates. Look for the gueros. They are supposed to be strangers, so they better tip you. Never refuse a tip from the blonde ones, but don't let them touch you.

Years pass and you're a woman now. This is what the eyes say on the walks home from the corner store. Sometimes men whistle. Sometimes they vocalize. You never give the satisfaction of eye contact. You have three knives on you. One by your side, one in your dangling earring and another in your boot. These are the material possessions that bring you peace of mind. You run errands for Madre during the day. She's always tired, always in bed, but she says it is a phase for her. The TV light radiates on her smile lines and worry lines. She asks you where your sister is. Is she out dancing? ¿Dónde está? Is she at the library finding new books to read? ¿Dónde está mi hija? Soledad has been missing for two months.

You have talked to every single person in your neighborhood. You roughed up a couple of men who attempted to flirt with you when you asked them for information. One of them grabbed you by the waist and sniffed your ponytail, so you pierced into the middle of his hand with the blade in your earring. You cleaned the knife on your pant leg and asked him to talk. This was a power you were growing into. The other man asked you to listen to him. Neither of them knew who your sister was or who made her vanish from this tierra. There are rumors of a bus taking women away. That is all he knew. The wounded man, bleeding and screaming, wailed at you about his kids at home. You told him to be better. Take care of those bebés and help his mujer at home. *Be better, hombre.*

Even though it's the middle of summer, you wear all black layers so you won't be seen en la noche and because you are mourning. During your investigation of the neighborhood, you run into your hermana's ex-boyfriend. You shove him against coral painted walls. He makes a simple statement about the way you wear your eyeliner.

"Have you seen Soledad?"

"I haven't seen her since we broke up."

"Have you heard anything about women disappearing?"

He scratches his face and pink skin exposes itself.

"There's a rumor about the local bus driver. Supposedly, he takes women to factory job interviews in the morning, but he never brings them back."

Soledad was looking for employment because the restaurant she worked at was shut down. Your mom was working less and you were having very little luck finding somewhere to make money. Do you think she went to El Paso to find a job, mija? Creo que sí mamá.

Soledad's ex shows you what stops the bus makes. The bus is painted like the Lineas de Juárez. Green and blanco como el flag pero sin la sangre. He tells you everyone knows about the buses, but they're too afraid to say shit. In the morning, before the sun has shown up, you walk to the corner of Calle Cactus and Dalia. The second stop for the bluffing bus. The bright green bus arrives on time and you get on. You shake for a matter of seconds and look up at the driver. As you step on, you see another woman on the bus and you calmly ask her to get off. You grab for the knife in your boot and you caress the blade against the man's Adam's apple. You apologize to the woman as she steps off. "Que Dios te bendiga." This is the only thing you can think to say.

You drag the man out. He is small. He has a gold chain with a cross around his neck. The belt looped around his waist has a buckle with gold flakes glistening against the sun forming a skinny line on the horizon. You are confused by his willingness to come along. He tries to introduce himself so you slice a shallow line into his neck. He doesn't say a word after that. Inside the house, you tape him up to a chair and close the blinds. Madre's TV is loud and you know she won't get up. You go to her room and kiss her hands. You tell her to let you know if she needs anything. You step back out to the trapped man. You grab his face. Your fingers digging into his cheeks.

"You drove those women away. You drove them away from their families. Ya no existen en esta tierra because of you. "

He spits at you. It oozes on the side of your cheek. You wipe it off and slap him repeatedly on the cheek with the full force of your body. He coughs out blood and looks up at you.

"I need income, niña. I have mouths to feed. I have grandchildren. Look in my wallet. I carry them with me todo el tiempo."

You are tempted to dig through his pockets, but for money to give to Madre. You place a strip of duct tape over his mouth. You spit at his face and then go check on Madre. She ate the soup you made for her. She asks you for water. You fill up two glasses for her and place them on her nightstand. As soon as your sister was gone for more than 48 hours, you started figuring out how to provide for your mom. You stole food from the grocery store. You sold stuffed animals on the border.

One night, on your way home, you passed the giant pecan tree in the middle of the neighborhood. A pecan landed on your head and when you cracked it open, there were rounded sprinkles inside. You opened more, one of them had honey inside and another had pomegranate seeds inside. The last pecan you picked up had confetti inside and a photograph. It was of you and Soledad. She made bunny ears behind your head. You both screamed CHEESE at the same time. You covered in penguins. Soledad covered in candy canes. You couldn't breathe or scream. You knew Soledad was gone.

After kissing Madre on the forehead, you go back to the trapped man and kick his chair over. You reach for his wallet and take out the photo of his grandchildren.

"I'm keeping this. I will pray for them. You can't do shit for them while you're in purgatory. ¿Me entiendes?"

You reach for the knife in your boot. You place it between your teeth while you pick the fallen man up. His hair thick between your fingers. You tilt his head back and he looks into your eyes. You twist his head around and to the side. You press the knife against the side of his head and his ear plops off into the palm of your hand. He screams beneath tape. You hold the ear between your teeth and grab his hair. You start to slice and rip some of his hair out. Once you're done cutting off his hair, you place the ear inside his wallet.

"You will be trapped in a purgatory. You will sit in a cell and you will listen. You will listen to the mothers praying at night for their kids to come back. You will feel what they are going through until you deteriorate."

You are shaking and tired. You take the photograph of his grandchildren and tear it in half. You drag him outside. You with your knives. Him with his ear in his wallet and his body taped to the chair. Blood follows you both to the pecan tree. You knock on the trunk, take the man's shirt collar and throw him on his side.

"Did you know? If you put your ear to the ground, the tree will tell you the history of this neighborhood."

The man is crying now. You're crying too. You grab the photo of you and Soledad and crumple it in your hand. His crying stops and he starts laughing.

"Can you hear the joke too?"

You could never bring yourself to lie on your side and listen. You caress through your hair and start to braid it while you wait for the roots to grab him. It's only a matter of seconds before you're both gone.

MORENA

I want to talk about my brown skin. I have to talk about it. My ability to travel through shades and spectrums is incomparable. I don't get red like a frustrated pale walker in the middle of a Macy's. The internet advertised a different price and things are never easy. I become deeper browns. I become enriched with the blanket of the poor. Those women who wear the coat of bronze as a status symbol of vacations could never sit with me.

CURLS

I obsess over the top of my head because it has never been a place of peace. My curls are geometric half-moons with a hint of coconut. They sleepwalk toward the sky while I experience dreams of a small empty house that only exists inside my mind. Follicles jump off to mimic ghosts of ancient insects. Oils entwine into the knots and strays. I wake up in a static mess of lush genetics and fallen strands on my pillow. This is the DNA I leave behind as circumstantial evidence for resisting a tame head of hair.

ENOJADA

If somebody asks me where I'm from or corners me to guess my ethnicity, I remember their faces and think about punching their throats when I'm taking a bath to relax. They bleed from their noses as part of the hex and one clump of hair falls out of their head. One patch of hair because I am merciful. I wear dangling elegant earrings when I take baths. I read books by people of color in the bath. I listen to my pulse like Amy Hempel told me to every once in a while and smile about the times I reacted con fuerza in defense of my existence.

TAROT

Mom read tarot for the loud ladies next to both sides of our building. She hid it from the Jehovah's Witnesses whenever we went to the halls on occasional Sundays and she explained to me that it was just a game. I walked into the kitchen and I saw the Death card face side up on the table. I cried before I went to sleep because this surely meant my mom picked the card of her demise. I prayed to god for no ghosts and good hair, but most of all, I prayed that it would let my mother live to see me learn her crafts.

COLORADO

The jugs filled with tempera paint weighed more than I was used to, but I was determined. I carried the blue paint in my backpack. The yellow in my left arm. The red in my right hand. I drew pictures of him. The ladies in the neighborhood swooned and became shy when they saw his short blonde curls and blue eyes. My crayon art depicted him as a headless man with blood bursting from the neck. I got a hold of giant permanent markers from the teen boy who always waved at my sister. I walked with a purpose and I kicked on the apartment door. I let myself in. He was sleeping on the mattress in the living room. I started by taking the markers and writing "NO" along the doors and the walls. I wrote a giant "NO" on his stomach and he woke up. I filled the room over and over with the word "NO." He asked me what I was doing. I'm a kid, I said. I'm a kid. I screamed it. I showed him the photos I drew of his head. I unzipped my backpack and uncapped the jug of blue tempera paint. I poured it on the mattress and soaked the carpet and my hands. I tossed the empty container across the room. He tried to touch me and I screamed "NO." I took the red tempera paint and I poured it on myself. I took the yellow and I stomped on the container. The yellow paint flowed out as my mom opened the door to the apartment.

In memories of Colorado, my mother is missing. I ride around the apartment complex on a yellow and orange tricycle. My sister Vero is cleaning the apartment and tells me to stay out until she's done. She's playing songs by a woman named Alanis. I know the lyrics because she's played the album over and over. As I sing along, the anger I can gather from my own voice pushes me to pedal faster and faster until I can no longer feel gravity.

I kept to myself. I collected ladybugs in a cake pan. Mud was the first layer. Grass was the second. I marked lines across and vertically and placed each ladybug into a numbered quadrant. I placed a window screen over the pan and left the ladybugs out overnight. The next morning, some of them died, others were barely alive. I wanted to tell my sister. I wanted to demand a funeral. I dumped the farm behind the apartment complex and prayed for the struggling ladybugs to continue their lives without me.

Vero said I needed religion so, she asked the upstairs neighbors for help. They were Jehovah's Witnesses. The youngest boy was partnered with me. He read from a mustard yellow book and asked me about the morals of every story. I told him I didn't care. I only wanted to play *Killer Instinct*. His eyes widened and he told me he could beat the game without losing a life. I asked him to prove it and he did. We ate waffle shaped cereal and played video games instead of reading from the mustard book.

Summer was over and school started again. I was pulled aside for tutoring. Spanish was my first language, but not the official language for the school system. The tutor held flashcards up for the words "heavy" and "light" and asked me to repeat after her. The word "light" confused me. I didn't understand how the feather in the picture brought me light. All I could think about was whether or not the white feather was plucked from a bird or if someone happened to find it in the grass.

I had dreams of my mother. She took me to Zacatecas. On cobblestone roads, we rode the bus to a women's prison. The prison was lit by candles. My mother held my hand and then gave me away to a woman in a cell. I had dreams of the blonde man being dragged into luminous rooms. When I tried to look inside, I only saw buildings collapsing into moths.

Winter covered Denver in fluffy snow. I waited at the bus stop in my psychedelic purple windbreaker. I swore I could see the individual patterns of the snowflakes before they melted into my palms. This was around the time I believed leprechauns could be captured in cups of glue and glitter. It was around the time a girl defended me by lying to the class. Someone came up and punched me in the chest. That was the lie. I was accused of being infatuated with a boy. I sobbed into my hands. The injustice I felt came from alienation. I was the new girl in class. They didn't even know me.

Winter led me to build my first snowman. He was short and lumpy. I named him Arturo. I stayed with

Tía Lola who collected my baby teeth and put me in karate class. She lived with her girlfriend Isabella, who cackled while dancing at birthday parties and at men who were afraid of her. They loved each other, but they fought a lot too. One night, while I was trying to get comfortable on the couch, Isabella threw an iron across the living room while screaming at my tía. She smashed a lamp into the ground. She slammed her palms against the kitchen table over and over. I'm still not sure who owed them money or if they owed someone money, but Isabella screamed "I am going to teach those motherfuckers a lesson!" She came out in baggy navy blue sweats, a beanie covering her head and a goatee drawn onto her face. She clutched onto a baseball bat and stormed out of the apartment. I hid under a blanket after she left. Days later, I stopped living with them and moved back to El Paso.

In El Paso, we moved into an apartment with Vero and her boyfriend. This is where my mother reappears into my memory. She had recently given birth to my youngest sister Magdalena who I was meeting for the first time. The blonde man with blue eyes showed up at the door. I froze and the only form of defense I could come up with was to growl. He ignored me and I was thankful. I held my breath as he walked past me and up the steps to see his daughter. I followed. He smiled at the small creature as she clasped his finger with her tiny hand. That was the last time I saw him. He walked out on my mother and my little sister. Even in my mother's heartbreak, I whispered loudly to my sister. I promised her I would take full responsibility in never telling her what her father was.

THE PULSE BETWEEN DIMENSIONS AND THE DESERT

Sylvia shuffled through her pockets and only felt a crisp dollar bill. Flaca and Morena had dropped her by the bus stop. They wanted to drink and dance to cumbias in Juárez. Sylvia had to go home. She just had a baby girl five months back. She named the infant after herself: Sylvia Estella. When people asked her: "¿Dondé está el papa de la bebé?" she would simply answer with "El culo se murió" to deter them. The wrath of her mamá was creeping into the forefront of Sylvia's mind. Her ma, Lupe, worked at a Levi's factory every day of the week and was calm while watching her telenovelas en la casa, but when Sylvia fucked up, Lupe was not one to be subtle about the repercussions of the fuck up. Lupe had a stack of chanclas in the small closet of the house, Sylvia swore. Her stomach gurgled as she looked into the window of the bakery.

"Hola, mija."

El viejito smiled as his eyes followed her to the counter. "Necesito cambio para el bus, por favor."

She straightened out the dollar bill which she had folded into a small clumpy square on her short walk to the shop. The little man tugged at the dollar and gave her change from his blue apron pocket.

"¿Tienes hambre, mija?"

Sylvia's belly announced itself in the empty shop. "¿Tiene pan dulce?"

The depth of brown in his eyes looked into hers. The display was empty, except for a handful of donuts. He nodded and headed to the back of the shop. He handed her a sweet loaf of bread that reminded Sylvia of the turtles she would catch with her cousin when she and Lupe visited LA back in the day. Sylvia ate the sugar shell pattern off the top of the fluffy bread and stashed the bottom portion in her pocket to give to the gutsy pigeons outside.

It started with trauma. Nothing sci-fi about it. No heavenly attributions. Just straight up time travel powers caused by trauma.

I was digging around the couch, looking for coins. We watched as the adults played "Quarters" with tequila and tiny glasses. I snuck into the kitchen, found the apple juice and grabbed the mini glass cups. One had Benjamin Franklin on it because my oldest sister's boyfriend bought it and said "Ay pues, electricity is my shit" and the other one had "Selena Forever" on it, in lovely purple cursive. As the volume of the adults elevated into more and more laughter, I poured the apple juice into the glasses and told my little sister Ruby the rules. We had to make the coins bounce into the glasses before we could drink and begin our battle as Orchid and Spinal in *Killer Instinct*. We missed two or three times before the coins finally plunged their histories into the apple juice and we sipped and dripped with stickiness on the sides of our mouths.

I woke up before any of the adults, surrounded by lavender walls. The air was thick with musk and fluctuations of alcoholic puffs of breath. The screen door squeaked open and shut. Clicks echoed as it rested back into its frame. I walked out of the bathroom and saw you. I saw you, so I tried to run to Ruby. I wanted to lie next to her and smell the baby shampoo in our hair strands. I wanted to wake her up and tell her about the dream I had: It was raining. We went digging for gems. She wore my turquoise sweater with the black squiggles on it and I wasn't even mad. You caught me, gripped my hair and those harsh hands turned my face toward yours. The power struggle that made me stop praying. You were an authority figure I often thought about suffocating. My back hit the bathroom tile. I thought about all the people who find you charming. I closed my eyes. A loud POP went off and I posed as though I was in the womb again. I felt a layer of warmth on me. As I opened my eyes, your body collapsed. Red fluid molecules flooded the air. I screamed and I screamed and then there was just darkness.

Sylvia stepped into the cooling evening. Her pockets jingled with her step by step by step. Graffiti embraced the payphone booth. Sylvia aligned her back against the phone booth's panel. The tone stopped and Lupe told her that Estelita was asleep. She better get home soon or she would raise Estelita to be a nun. "Ay, Mamá, espero al bus."

Sylvia trembled and hung up on Lupe. The barrel of a shotgun rested on her cheek. A gringo with eyes como el cielo and hair el mismo color like the heroes in telenovelas was holding the weapon.

"Do you understand English?"

He spoke slowly.

Sylvia thought of the white puta she beat the shit out of for telling her that she sounded ugly when she spoke Spanish.

"Yes, a little."

Tobacco particles escaped from his spit. He told her not to scream and pushed her toward a white mustang. Sylvia thought of sharks. Mustangs were sharks of the freeway. Gringos were loan sharks. Gringos were the reiteration of the times she'd been called a wetback. Gringos grinned as though they owned the fucking universe.

She settled into the leather seat.

Lupe was going to be pissed.

Estelita would never forgive her.

She should have kept track of Alfonso.

Child support would have helped Estelita.

"Ey, how old are you?"

His fingers invaded her crunchy curls. Sylvia could barely think and whispered a number.

"Ey, that's cool. You're my sixteen year old girlfriend now, okay?"

Sylvia refused to cry. Era dura because she had to be. It had come to Sylvia's attention that women in Juárez meant nada, so what, if another Chicana went missing?

Blue and red lights radiated through the windows. The shark car stopped. A police officer tapped at the window. This was one of the only times Sylvia felt relief in seeing a cop.

The blood is gone. My body heat contains itself underneath a blanket decorated with the sun, la luna and the stars. My lungs expand with the crisp air flowing into me as I emerge from beneath the blanket. Candlelight illuminates the small woman who comes into the room to feel my forehead and caress my hair with warm wet cloth. The smell of spices from the kitchen and the scent of her rose oil bring me comfort.

"No se que pasó mija, pero con el favor de Dios, tiene su salud."

I call her my new mother. Her name is Rosalina. We settle into a desolate town. Clusters of lonely clouds stick themselves on top of the sky. Stars swim and drown in between the nothingness en la noche. The residents are righteous and outrageous in their insights. Floral patterns settle over their chests, over their hearts and the softness of their human bodies. In Palomar, we tell each other stories to pass the time. The stories always evolve into rumors about the people in the town.

The viejita who lives on the corner en la casa azul can tell the future. She has an old parrot who gives her formulas for the future. No one has ever stepped into her house, but I looked through the window once and I saw números in white paint all over her purple walls. I heard the pajarito demand galletas on the way to Delia's. Delia sells churros and eggs to most of us in town. I heard the little bird shout

"Uno!"

"Dos!"

"Cuatro!!"

The pajarito said these three numbers slowly and then went into accelerated number shouting. I thought maybe he just never learned how to properly count.

I fell asleep in Palomar and I woke up in El Paso en el futuro. Newspapers indicated 2010. In Palomar, it was 1952. I didn't have any papers so I cleaned houses for ladies with big hair and overpowering fragrances. I worked with five other women. Cassandra was my favorite. She was blunt and adequately harsh on the white women we worked for. Behind their backs, we laughed about how they looked orange because even though they had money, they could never be melanin rich.

Cassandra was my first kiss and my first fuck. We lived together through passing seasons. We raised succulents and laughed at each other as often as we could in between the reality of economic circumstances and our introspections. One night, after falling asleep in her arms, I woke up alone in 1974.

With the windows rolled down, Sylvia looked up at the policía and out to the pavement, where she calculated her first grave would be.

"Young lady, what's your boyfriend's name?" The gringo had his grip on her wrist and squeezed harder.

"I don't know."

Sylvia saw psychedelic spots and her head began to burden her shoulders.

"Get out of the car."

The police officer pulled her out. The last time policía interacted with her, he followed behind her and her hermano before he finally searched the both of them on the basis that they were "acting suspicious".

Sylvia stumbled and breathed in the smog and the heaviness of her mortality.

"We were patrolling the area and someone called and reported what happened."

Sylvia sifted through her thoughts and the viejito popped into it.

The nearest bar is a miniature structure packed with men portraying masculinity behind mustaches. I drench my fragility in tequila until I can't feel the hot tears possessing my face. Someone addresses me by "mija" so, I stare into him. He simply offers me pan dulce. I chuckle at him. He has a brown paper bag with sweet bread in it and here he is, at this macho bar in his vaquero gear.

"I know I am in the past. I can tell by the fucking cars and the way you dress and I know she hasn't even existed yet."

I tell him about Cassandra's messy hair and her perfect eyebrows that had to be on point before she went out. He sighs and hands me a concha.

"Come esto. You need to hydrate mija."

I chug water as he explains the science behind creating perfect pan dulce. We step into the parking lot where the sun shower from the morning dissipated back into the sky. The rhythm of my step stops. Someone has a grip on the back of my shirt's collar.

He shows me a small knife.

He whispers something about being able to fix me.

He says something about me being dirty, una cochina.

Pasty vaquero puffs up.

An alcohol induced altercation has me on the gravel. All I hear after that is "Run!"

I know that Mister Pan Dulce is hurt, but I have to run.

I run myself sober and the next morning, I wake up hungover in 1993.

Sylvia didn't look behind her. She could feel the egos disappear to the station. She spit the lump in her throat onto the ground. She clenched her fists, breathed deep and thought of Estelita. Walking to the bakery, she felt her pocket and the sweet bread wasn't there anymore. She ran to look inside the shop and the viejito wasn't there. She slapped the glass with the force of her body until her arms and hands stung.

Inside the bakery, el viejito only had a second to recognize his limbs erasing themselves from time. Soon after, the donuts popped out of space and back into stardust. The pink spinning seats turned into nothingness. The infrastructure of pipes and little cucarachas blipped and blinked out of vision. Sylvia collapsed onto her knees in between yellow lines that were deleting themselves as though a backspace bar was clicking them off of the asphalt.

* * *

On the bus ride home, Sylvia fell asleep and had a dream she was tripping over the border of Juárez and into El Paso. She looked behind her and saw the women who could never go home to their hijos or hijas.

The first time I killed a man, I felt satisfaction. I knocked on the apartment window to my old room after putting a hole in his head and seeing the miniature version of myself disappear. Screams came from the bathroom, but I got Ruby's attention. Ruby opened the window and told me she liked my curls. I asked her to give me the Super Nintendo control and I showed her the combos to press so she could be invincible as Orchid.

CHURCH BUSH

Sex advice filtered into my cranium from hidden Cosmo magazines. Men compared their balls to baby birds and licked spaghetti sauce off of nipples when they got home from work. There were thousands of manners in pleasing a man. I wasn't interested in making men moan. I read through the magazines because I knew I wasn't supposed to. I licked the perfume samples. I circled the faces that struck me. I cut out these faces and stuffed them into my pillow in hopes of seeing them when I fell into sleep. Wet dreams delivered themselves to me in black and white. I avoided living with the sensation between my legs at all costs. I crossed my legs and took in deep breaths until I thought about something else.

The Baptist church provided me with pamphlets of sexual defiance. You are a piece of tape. The more times you stick yourself to others, the less you will stick to your soul mate. You are a piece of candy. If some random man sucks on the candy, then stuffs you back into the wrapper, you become a sticky mess for your perfect gem of a future husband. Don't get sucked on and don't tape yourself to boys in class. You don't sin on Saturday and then get forgiveness on Sundays. Jesus has no time for a promiscuous and pious dichotomy. I was neither pious nor promiscuous. The Sunday school teacher still made us all sign an oath and stuff it into a box called the Virginity Package. She claimed she would deliver it to God in the coming weeks.

Puberty created enchantment for older men with ramen noodle hair and teeth made for the gods. Puberty established shame. My period allowed me to draw the curtains for drama and made me feel like shit. Pads like diapers stuck to the bridge of my panties because I was petrified of tampons getting stuck inside me. This signifier of a fertile womb gushed out and sexuality remained sequestered in the deeper parts of my teenage brain. In public, my mom would shout at me when she saw a viejita who was slouching down to her knees. In her boxers and chanclas with socks, she yelled that my frame would hunch over like that if I didn't straighten my back. No man would love my slouch or my sloppiness. Brush your hair and smile. When we got home, she apologized. Her mom used to say those words to her. She regretted saying them to me.

I trembled when I heard songs about fucking on the radio. Church created a safety barrier from having to think about sex in a gratifying manner. Waiting until marriage was key. The concept of two virgins creating magical bodily connections on their wedding night was a prominent conversation at Sunday school. No one said anything about the messiness and malfunctions. No one described the odors or fart noises. Most of the time, I didn't care about my sexuality, but I had my moments. I cared when I saw Kate Winslet naked in *Titanic* at the Dollar Theater on Paisano. I cared when I settled a couple of fingers inside myself during winter time to warm my hands at first, only to wake up to pruned fingers after a nap. I cared when I kissed Laura as a dare at a church retreat. I cared when Rosa laughed and pointed at my crotch during a sermon.

My underwear was too big and the skirt I had on was too tight. My bush overcame the tightness of my skirt and created a puffy cloud over my pubic mound. I tried to press it down before we had to shake hands with new members of the church. Pat, pat, pat. I was frantic and continued to smack the fluff. The cloud remained. When I got home, I shut the blinds and combed through it. I gooped hair gel on it and tried to flatten it out. I sat in my purple fold-out chair with no calcones on and a cool breeze whispering to my crotch from the air-conditioner. Mom walked in and yelled something like "Ay, mija, this isn't the Panocha Monologues. You can't just sit with your legs open like that." My face burned and mom handed my underwear over to me.

"Mamá, I don't think I'm normal."

"Why not, mija?"

I couldn't bring myself to mutter a word. She sat with me in silence and patted my head when she was done braiding my hair.

"Take a warmth bath. Wash the gel out of her or him or whatever gender kids are giving their panochas these days. I'll bring you some tea and I will turn on the *X-Files* for you okay?"

Sunday school became fun because of Laura. We sat next to each other in the second story of the church and documented the number of women with anti-gravity hair. The average number being seventy-two. There was one Sunday where we both brought a bottle of hairspray and tried to give each other anti-gravity hair. Her hair was curly like mine so I decided to make her head into a nest instead. She braided my hair up and sprayed it to a crisp. We ran to the second story of the church and tried to hold back laughter as the pastor discussed white lies becoming habitual.

"Do you ever lie to people?"

Laura asked me this while tracing the curls in her nest with her finger. I told her I wasn't sure what I would have to lie about. She took out her notebook and jotted down the number of people with gray hair below us. She counted the redheads. She surveyed for anti-gravity hair last. When the sermon was done, she handed me a piece of paper and told me not to read it until I got home. I couldn't wait to get home. I ran up to my room and opened her note. It said "I like you." Mom knocked on the door and asked me what I wanted for lunch. I held the note between my hands. I asked her to come in.

"Mamá, someone left me a note. It says 'I like you'."

She smiled and snatched the note from my hand.

"Do you like them back?"

My heart was thumping louder and louder. I tell her yes, but it's a girl. Mom, it's a girl who likes me and I like her back.

"Okay then. You both like each other. That's very sweet. What do you want for lunch?"

I hugged my mom and my belly growled with butterflies and hunger.

The next Sunday, I saw Laura and she looked away when I waved at her. I asked her to sit with me upstairs. I remember sprinting up the steps. I got there before she did and once she made it to the bench I simply said "YES." I wrote "I like you too" into her notebook and erased it so the people above us could not see it. I motioned for a high-five and she smiled and we high-fived. I smiled through the sermon, although I can't remember what the pastor was saying. The church felt comfortable and safe for once. It was because of the church that I met Laura.

LA LOBA

Darkness has shifted the desert air. I watch. The distance is enough. She cannot hear me. She's wearing a red gown that drags behind her as she inspects the environment. She starts a fire. She's wearing the mask of a quetzal with iridescent green feathers and a tiny yellow beak. She mixes mescaline powder and water into a bowl. She stirs with her hand and rolls orbs of green, lifts her mask and swallows. She waits in silence.

She is not afraid of the creatures burrowed underneath the terrain. She has not looked over her shoulder to gaze at me. Women find me in their deepest moments. I form into wolf and let them pet me or hold me. When I first appear, I have no facial features. My face is a dark oval with silver hair lining where my head begins and where my hips end. I have frightened some into tears. I have terrified others because they thought of me as a monster. I am locked into a code. I can only transform for those who are truly lost. Otherwise, Las Manos in the desert erupt from beneath the earth and take them under. Fingers stretch up and petrichor invades the atmosphere. Todos los animales scurry away. Stars fade out of the sky and the eyes of my ancestors glow red as they watch these final moments. Las Manos are merciful. The captured are lulled to sleep before they disappear. I have seen Las Manos cradle those who expired.

The bird woman has collapsed beside the fire. She's digging into stubborn dirt. She isn't here for anything spectacular. These are the things she says to me. She's here because of her job and because of a man. She is here because she has floated between identities for years and years. She's fucking exhausted. She cleans up after families who pigeonhole her. She forgot to clean one of the bathrooms. She forgot to dust the trophies accumulated by cushioned children. She forgot to respond as though her entirety was dependent on them. Then, there's this man. She didn't apologize for calling him in the middle of the night while he fucked around. He said it out loud. She was not important to him. Infidelity wasn't the final line. He told her she was nothing. She doesn't feel sorry for herself. She is just tired. She is going to nap with the nopales and La Loba looking after her. She is going to let the sun wake her up as the drugs wear off.

Dust devils collect the whispers and final thoughts belonging to women and children of the sun. I lead the lost away from the depths of the desolation to an interstate or close to a horizon with twinkling grids. This is as much as I can do.

LADY
MESCALINE

Via destiny, you sat next to your best friend, Laura, in the back of science class. Prior to text messages and social media, passing notes on college ruled paper sufficed. She scribbled fast and slid a corner of torn lines to you. It said, "YOU ARE XENA." It was caps lock serious. You looked up to Xena and could not fathom someone looking up to you. Laura smiled. Dimples left craters in her cheeks.

The first time you saw a crater, it was a tourist trap and the silence magnified as you stepped further toward the bottom. There were no conversations between your family members. Settled into a picnic booth, you looked into the crater and felt heavy.

In moments of panic, you lash out. Pillows are the casualties. You were settled into bed with the love of your life and the cartoon you usually laughed at made you cry. Tu amor let you be. He knew the story. The story of the step-father who showed you no mercy. The father of your brother and sisters. You were his target. You remember every feature of his face.

Your two days off came with perfect timing. This gave you enough time to plot revenge. One time your sister called to ask him why you hated him. He told her he didn't know. Hate is simplistic. You have dragged him along with you. He is chewed gum in your hair or chewed gum that you shit out after seven years. He is the filament of hair on your head that grows silver and brown, silver and brown. The moment you notice it, you rip it out. Sometimes, family members slip and talk about him. He's created more children and you pray to an echo that he leaves them alone since they are biologically his. You are crystal on why you weren't the exception.

Under the influence of mescaline, you looked into a mirror and saw accuracy in the depiction of your being. Your hair strands extended above you, glowing and vibrating. Your eyes traveled through your timeline and grabbed those moments when people were kind. Laura was there with her notebook paper. Your cousin Omar was there with a water pistol. The bruja Letty, who told you anger was a valid emotion, was there too. They sat at the picnic table in silence as you caressed the bottom of the crater with the hands that crawled away from a man who could never understand why you refuse to forgive him.

ESMAI

Discs shift beneath the earth. Your dog is cautious, her eye on the photographs swaying from side to side, tapping louder and louder against the hollow wall. She whimpers, so you hold onto her. You pet her lightly and scratch behind her floppy ears. You kiss her head. Your back is throbbing from a 12 hour shift the day before. If everything crumbles, you hope you can dig your way out and find pain killers before your crushed softness sees the light at the end of a hollow tube. You run to the kitchen and swallow a pill dry. The dog is still watching the picture frames slow dance. Multiple family photos. Three of you and your mom. One of you, Great Grandma, Abuela, Mom and your sister. Four generations with crowns of flowers on their heads.

Mom calls and tells you Great Grandma has passed. She was surrounded by her Chihuahuas. They barked and howled as her breathing slowed. The three of them jumped off of the bed and woke your Tía. Tía ran to your bisabuela's room and the Matriarch of the family was gone. Her name was Martha Velo. She represented the stubborn and resilient lineage you belong to. You ask Mom if she's okay. She says yes, but she wishes she hugged her grandma harder the last time she saw her. She tells you to take care of your plants. You hang up and make sure your plants are still living.

The earth doesn't stop, but your apartment stops shaking. An apocalypse means wearing a quality pair of combat boots, underwear, pants, plus, a reliable sense of direction, hydration and packing vitamin-filled foods. You step outside. The air smells like skunk. The clouds expand into wisps in the yellow sky. The upstairs neighbors are sucking madly on their cigarettes. The brunette looks down at you and sends you an eyebrow. If this were the end of the planet, you'd kill them. There's no way they wouldn't kill you and Spatula and then eat her. You look at the sky and whisper to Great Grandma that you are just kidding.

Spatula is on her hind legs, watching you and wishing she could use her mouth to say thank you for making the shaking room stop. Spatula thinks about her squirrel toy, sniffs it out and shakes the squirrel by the neck. Spatula's a good girl. Her tail wags when those words pop into her head. She gallops into the room and finds a spot on the bed. Stuffing as confetti settles into the carpet. Spatula huffs. The ground vibrates for five, four, three, two, one. You run inside and inspect the apartment. The living room and kitchen look okay. You look into your room and grab your chest. Red splotches start forming on your neck. There's a napping astronaut beside Spatula. Or maybe the astronaut is dead? You're not sure. Spatula doesn't seem to mind. Her head is nuzzled on the astronaut's thigh. You knock on the helmet and clear your throat.

"Excuse me. Excuse me, astronaut person… hopefully a person… you're in my apartment and I would appreciate it if you left…please?"

You shake their shoulder and tap on the helmet once again. The astronaut springs up and turns toward you. A green button on the neck of the suit opens the helmet and it's your own face looking at you. You jump back.

"Hello, Esmai. I know this is fucked up."

Spatula's tail thumps against the bed and she goes over to lick the astronaut's face.

"I don't understand."

"Who's a good girl? You are such a pretty puppy!"

The astronaut is captivated by Spatula. She grabs Spatula's ears and makes them dance. She kisses Spatula on the head. This makes the situation more palatable, but your gut still feels uneasy. She turns to you.

"Hello, I'm Maribel. I'm a time travel agent from portal Q2786 and I am here as a fugitive of sorts."

You rub your forehead. Purple and gold spots begin to form in your line of vision. Sitting is your best option and it's a relief on your back.

"Explain."

"Of course. You are the first version of myself that I have found, by the way. This is really neat."

She presses a blue button on the wrist of the suit and it starts disappearing from her body. A tiny cube forms and she places it into a case attached to a silver belt around her waist.

"As a travel agent, I was part of an agency that searched for lost kids from other portals and dimensions that started on this version of earth. Kids go missing everyday right? Well, my department investigated disappearances that were never solved. Most times, the kids were deceased, but sometimes we found lost kids stuck in between time portals. If we got there in a reasonable amount of time, we could rehabilitate the child and send them to a foster family in a different version from their earth of origin. People can't survive long in between time portals so, if we were too late, they'd be deceased."

Maribel's hair is silver. You notice that even the hair on her arm is silver. Her speech patterns are similar to your own. Are you really in your own room? Are you locked up somewhere with this dream sequence looping through you?

"So, how does that make you a fugitive? What's the point of finding me…you?"

"There's a political campaign against multi-dimensional travel. They are marketing through xenophobia, claiming the kids my department has rescued should be left for dead. They claim the kids should not be allowed on an earth from which they were not born. The government is killing agents from my department off in secret, one by one. I'm not the only agent in trouble. There are others looking for multidimensional versions of themselves, too. I don't know how many of us are left, but I know they killed one of us off. They got to her before I could."

Your palms are soaking and the pain in your back is reaching up toward your shoulders. Is this the apocalypse you dreamed about? You dreamed of zombies and a bright emerald gun as your weapon of choice. You dreamed of sinkholes swallowing earthlings' whole. The only way to fight back was to build a net connected to the sky. A little moleskine with the list of apocalyptic dreams is sitting on the lavender dresser next to your bed.

"Okay, are you here to take me with you? Can I have a cool shrinking cube thing?"

"I have extra suits, yes. I brought enough for six others. I figured I would give my spiel and see where we go from there."

Overwhelming pain is settling in your head. Would you be able to leave your mom alone? She just lost Great Grandma.

"Maribel, I need to take a bath first."

The water stings against your skin. Tired bones against the yellow tub. With your head back, your hair spreads out and the earth is mute. You are considering traveling with yourself into other dimensions to find more versions of yourself so you can all hang out and survive together. You have scraps of paper hanging in front of the toilet in case you are taking a shit when the apocalypse comes. Push it out. Pull up your pants. Possibly use the shit as a weapon or a distraction.

Maribel might read your other apocalypse tips as she paces in your apartment. This brings you comfort and it makes you cringe at the same time. When you step out of the tub you look above you. There are red X's that you drew for every apocalyptic dream you were a part of. There are over one hundred markings.

"Maribel? I want to know more. I am someone with two jobs, a dog and a pile of debt. That's about all I have and I'm not sure I could make your trip easier. I am in a strange place."

Maribel digs through a rectangular navy bag, which jingles and dings as she shuffles through it. A quaint sky blue lizard crawls up Maribel's arm and leaps into her silver curls.

"That's Nebula. I received her as a gift for entering puberty. She's a feisty lizard queen. I think she's seven years old at this point."

"Is she your Spatula?"

"I guess so."

"Wait, so you got gifts for starting your period? I just got a box of giant pads and my mom warning me that tampons would take my virginity."

Maribel laughs and brings her hand out in a fist.

"I want to show you how we can survive."

She places a cube in your hand. This one is much smaller than the suit cube. A light emerges from its center.

"What's your favorite piece of art?"

"Right now, it's the *Space Empress* comics. I just finished reading *Interstellar Romance* and I haven't cried like that in a long time."

"Bring me the comic."

You shuffle through the piles of single issues on your floor and find it. She places the cube in your hand. You find the last page of *Interstellar Romance* and stare down at it.

"Hold my hand. Look at the pages and then look into the light."

You do. You are light. Maribel is waves of reds and blues. You can see yourself burst into atoms. You become rainbow particles and specks before you transform back into yourself. Maribel looks like swirls of glitter particles before her body puts itself back together. You see the Space Empress (Evangeline). She has been stuck on the planet Nexon for 10 years. Her lover (Benicio) just exploded into dust. He was a hologram, but Evangeline loved him as hard as she could. Evangeline speaks into an electronic journal. She tells the journal the date of Benicio's passing (January 22nd, 2410). She explains the details of their relationship from beginning to end. Once she's done recording their moments together, there are eight panels concentrating on Evangeline's face. She looks to the dark horizon and you see the red veins crossing paths in the whites of her eyes. Her mouth is open. She does not move. 90 years pass and an unfamiliar species (Hexaborgs) find Evangeline. The Hexaborgs cannot understand Evangeline's mother tongue. She cannot tell them about Benicio. The Hexaborgs scan Evangeline and place her in a sterile cell because her immune system is fragile. None of them seem to notice you and Maribel. You're terrified the Hexaborgs will inspect and isolate you both if they find out you are watching them. You know how this story finishes. You want to warn Maribel. You know what happens to Evangeline. She dies alone on this spaceship. In three pages, a Hexaborg finds her curled up under her bed surrounded by potted mini cacti and succulents. She becomes space dust and her particles float out of the cracks in the spacecraft. You are getting closer and closer to that last page. Your throat is tight and your eyes rumble with stinging tears. Maribel sees your tears and wipes them with her thumb. You get to the last page and she's right in front of you. Evangeline is thinking about her final moments with Benicio. With enthusiasm, Benicio explained some of the fruit available on his home planet. Fruits shaped like galaxy spirals that tasted so sweet, your gums ached and your belly danced. Fruits shaped like canoes with pink seeds inside that made you grow strands of pink hair on your head. Benicio's favorite fruit was called an atomic root. It was a miniscule sphere that glowed at night. The tiny roots on the orb attached themselves to your taste buds and injected refreshing citrus flavors into them. Evangeline is sitting on Nexon with Benicio and she caresses through the hologram in front of her. Benicio kisses Evangeline and for a moment his face disappears into hers. The panel shifts back into her sterile cell. You and Maribel approach the panel and she looks up. You run toward her and hold her. You can really feel this tiny woman in your arms. She embraces you back and you bring her head toward your chest so she can hear the organs inside you vibrating and keeping you alive. You kiss her head, help her into bed and tell her "Good night, Evangeline." You and Maribel arrange potted plants around her bed.

You are light and Maribel is green and red waves again. You pop into your room where Spatula and Nebula are napping on the bed. They both perk up and start running around the apartment, frantic and excited.

"That was amazing! We saw the Hexaborgs and Evangeline! Is this how you're going to keep running from the government?"

Maribel nods her head.

"I helped create the devices with my team. This is another reason the government wants us found. They want restricted access placed on our invention."

Maribel could be a powerful ally in an apocalypse. Maybe she's the version of you who is actually ready to endure the inevitable. She is made to survive. You leave the room to call your mom. You ask her if she's okay and she says yes, but you know she's lying. You get dizzy from the sadness you can hear in her voice. You tell her you love her and that you will talk to her tomorrow. You call your boss at job 1 and then job 2. You aren't going in this weekend.

Maribel stretches and yawns. She takes a note out of her pocket. It is one of your notes from the living room wall. She smiles as she reads the list.

"'In case of emergency do not call loved ones. Do not call them. DO NOT CALL THEM. Only call them if you want to say a quick goodbye and never contact them again.' Esmai, what is this obsession with an apocalypse?"

You blush. Your ears burn.

"I'm not blood moon apocalypse crazy. When it comes to the end of the world, I can only trust myself. I call myself apocalypse-lite"

Maribel laughs. You can't because you are serious.

"One night in October, I went to bed. I thought I was having a dream. I saw a hole in the side of my bedroom wall. I could see constellations and pulsating stars. I wanted to touch outer space. I walked through and couldn't breathe. I stopped thinking. I stopped existing. I disappeared from my home planet. Space people found me. They were special agents. I became enamored with making that my career."

Maribel has Nebula in her palm. She pets the lizard. The lizard jumps up onto her shoulder.

"I'm sorry, Maribel."

"It's okay."

"Maribel? What if I don't want to go with you? What then? Why don't we go somewhere together instead? I can take you to the desert. We can be tourists. The Grand Canyon is amazing. We can go to all the tourist traps and buy shitty food at gas stations. I'll buy you key chains for your space bag."

She smiles. Runs her small hands through her silver curls.

"Let's go to the art museum! It'll be my gift to you. Pick one piece and after we have travelled through it, I'll bring you home and I will leave."

Something about her leaving feels heavy in your chest.

Maribel is tapping her fingers together. You guess the taps are based on a song you will never hear. In case she does disappear for a long time, why not ask her to hang out? You can pretend to be twins. She yawns and you can't help but think that this is still a lucid dream. The ground trembles. Is it another earthquake? Spatula panics and runs under your feet. Maribel grabs her bag and rips the poster of galaxy clusters off of your wall. She is clutching the small glowing cube. She is going to run.

"Why don't you just pick a comic book? How do you even know what the fuck to do, surrounded by vast space? Won't you just die?"

You dig through the pile of comic books with super heroes displaying their muscles and strange perfection. Detective Lupe Santiago AKA Time Fatale has been a personal favorite character. She's unafraid and of course, she can stop time. She is acutely observant and could help Maribel figure out a solution other than running.

"Here. Go find this woman. She might be able to help you. If not, you can just blend in as a pedestrian. What's wrong with that?"

There's a loud bang on the door.

"On the count of three, we are coming in!"

Three large figures kick through the door and tear through the wall.

"Maribel Esperanza Mercado: You are under arrest for trespassing into time portals without proper authorization and for participating in the programming of a time travel device for the consumption of the American public."

Spatula frees herself from underneath you and starts barking. One of the officers aims his weapon at her. He pushes the trigger button. You tense up and jump in front of Spatula. There is a hole going through your belly. All you can do is scream. You continue to scream in tears as you watch your blood make streams on your thighs and collect into the carpet. You keep your body in front of the dog.

"Help her!"

Maribel reaches for you and one of the officers grabs her by the hair.

"Agent Mercado, please come with us. Our intent is not to hurt anyone."

"Help Esmai. Help her."

Maribel punches through the officer's helmet and spits in his eye. She grabs a piece of helmet shard and digs it into the officer's neck. The other two continue to watch Maribel and one of them scoffs.

"It's very simple. You are under arrest. Give us the device and come with us."

You tumble over. Your face is in the carpet. Spatula is nudging at your face. Should you whisper "I love you" to family members in hopes they will hear it as they place you underground? Can Great Grandma hear you right now? You feel guilty. Your mom will have no daughters left. Is this the pre-apocalypse on this version of earth? Has it all started with you? Maribel has handed over her bag. She's crying. You hope she will live for centuries.

"Esmai. I'm so sorry."

The officers watch as she places your potted plants around you. The succulents from great grandma. The cactus from your sister, Lucy. Tiny reminders of the desert that kept you connected to your family. Maribel caresses your face and holds you. Lucy gave you a cactus plant before you moved out of the house. It took her three hours to pick the right one. She picked a turquoise pot and decorated the edges of the pot with stick-on earrings she bought from the Dollar Store. The next day, she was gone. She was found in the middle of the desert. Your knees fell into cement after it was "officially" announced. You held onto the cactus and spines dug into your cheek. You prayed she walked out there in her sleep and that no one harmed her. Your mom came over and helped you pick the cactus spines out. She told you about the first time she realized how small she really was. We are specks in this mess. We are so miniscule, but we express ourselves with the magnitude of an entire galaxy. Maribel kisses your cheek and you can smell the essence of time travel escaping from her pores. She shuts your eyes.

"Go to sleep, apocalyptic friend."

ROSARIO

He walks up to me and asks me where I'm from. I ask him what he means. He says, you know what I mean. I tell him I was born in Los Angeles. He stands in front of me and asks where my parents are from. I say, my mom is from Mexico and my dad is from Guatemala. He tells me he knew I was an American woman because I speak English well. I tell him Spanish was my first language.

"You know what I mean."

He starts to speak to me in Spanish with a heavy gringo accent. I can smell his breath and his sweat. He's asking me if I know how to say 'hammer' in Spanish. What about 'warlock?' How do you say 'witch' in español? He looks me up and down and asks me for my phone number. I tell him to fuck off. He says he's a nice guy. He has money. He appreciates the beauty in a brown woman. I tell him to fuck off.

"I'm only complimenting you. You know what I really mean."

I don't feel like explaining myself to white boys anymore. I have mace attached to my keychain. I unlock the container. I snatch the glasses from his face and press down on the pepper spray button. I soak his face and he's screaming. I stomp his glasses under my sneakers and bolt away until I can't hear him scream anymore. That conversation gets older and older every time a white boy spits it out. Sometimes, I think about crushing their windpipes and slicing through their ankles with blades. I would never go that far, but thinking about it makes me feel better.

Blatant sexualization of my brownness makes me gag. I gag out of anger. I used to gag out of fear. At fifteen, three white boys surrounded me and complimented my skin color. They asked if my brown skin indicated dark nipples. They asked me if I shaved. They wanted to see.

"You know what we mean."

I thought they were joking so, filled with nerves, I laughed. One of them picked me up and I couldn't force myself off of him. He took me into an empty house. The other two followed and watched as the leader threw me on the ground. All you have to do is show us. We want to see what you look like naked. I didn't understand why. They told me I was exotic. It was supposed to be a compliment.

At fifteen, I used to look at myself in the mirror in strangely padded bras and loose underwear. I pretended that my skin was lighter. My hair was lighter. My eyes were lighter. I was someone else and I smiled. I never slouched. I stood tall as I waved at the brown girl on the other side of the mirror. The three white boys undressed me and saw what they wanted. They saw weakness. That's what I used to think.

They saw an object.

I know this now.

That's not how I want this to end. I have been told that forgiveness will make me feel better over and over again. I do not forgive. I have not forgiven them and this brings me peace of mind. There's power in my grudge. I do not hold myself responsible for the despicable shit white supremacy has served to me as a legitimate form of expression for white boys. I do not wish them peace. I do not wish them happiness. The most I could give them is a middle finger and spit on the ground at the sound of their names.

LAS MUJERES

Neri Guevara and Mya Soldado work together cleaning houses six times a week. Nine hours a day, they scrub the dead skin cells and grime of the fiscally privileged. Then, they go home, drink some tea and tell each other short stories about their past lives.

Mya was born in Guatemala City in 1967. She traveled to the states in 1990. She works to sustain herself and to send money to her son Rodolfo. She sends him money every month. He's in Guatemala with a baby girl (Natalia) and a pajarito (Lalo) to look after. He mails Mya a card with a different theme every month as a thank you.

For March: Sloths.

In April: Roses.

En el May: Pajaritos.

In June: Sand castles.

This month, Mya received a card with the Catedral Metropolitana in the center of the city and a photograph of Lalo on top of Natalia's head. In a yellow dress like limón, baby Natalia is showing gums and two top teeth. Her arms reach toward the sky in glee of Lalo's resting spot. Mya focuses on the fact that there are several framed photos of her in the background.

Mya sips on her tea then tells Neri: before this life, I was a messenger dove. Una mujer, perhaps a bruja, wearing a sheer black veil with velvet roses on it whispered mensajes to me and every morning, a scroll manifested in my nest for me to deliver. I delivered them to gente in front of la Iglesia de San Andrés Xecul. I transported the scrolls to locals, tourists, Abuelas, and children. The veiled woman whispered to me about lineage and solitude. Every morning, I heard the same message and every morning, I gave a scroll to someone new.

Neri stirs tea with her finger and tells Mya: before this life, I was a calavera possessed by the desert. In White Sands, New Mexico I collected crystals left behind by Martians on brief visits. They left the crystals as gifts for the living, but I calculated they were better fit for the dead. I walked on soft white sand in darkness with a crown of roses on my skull, but never ever left evidence of my wandering. During daylight hours, I sent twirls of wintry air to embrace the guest standing over me. Most ran away, others shut their eyes and kept shifting feet into the sand. The day a curious child decided to dig me up was the same day I passed away.

Neri was born in El Paso, Texas in 1992. She lost contact with her madre and padre on purpose. They aren't bad people, but they aren't good people either. Neri misses them in instances of panic. She locks herself in her room, hides under a blanket and cries until she has to emerge for oxygen. Her nerves shift from silence to on the fritz, but she takes her breaths in with depth. In public spaces, she runs to restrooms and covers her eyes with her hands and recites the countries she wants to see. Chile. Peru. France. Guatemala. South Korea. Indonesia.

Neri is up by six so she can catch the bus by seven. Mya wakes up around five to spend moments alone with her thoughts and her coffee. They became roommates after meeting on the Greyhound from El Paso to Denver. A viejito with gray eyes planted himself next to Neri. He took Neri's hand into his and asked her to let him take care of her. Viejito claimed he could love her. Mya snatched her hand away and scolded the viejito until he moved to another seat. Mya asked Neri if she was alone. Neri nodded and then retreated into sleep. The ride from El Paso to Denver took fourteen hours. Mya told Neri about her decision to move as a new start on perspective. Neri didn't say very much, but enjoyed the way Mya smiled when she talked about her son and the way her braided hair had curly escapees reaching out like tree roots grasping for earth.

Neri and Mya work with four other mujeres. Nayeli, with green eyes and a cackle that makes everyone else laugh during rides in the company minivan. Diana, who writes telenovela fan fiction and knows all the gossip happening in her family from Juarez, LA, and Albuquerque. Lupita, who wears red lipstick todos los días and takes a photo of her baby boy every morning with an imprint of her lips on his forehead. Yvonne with short pink hair and a tattoo of a rose on her forearm dedicated to her sister who passed away two years back.

Today, they are assigned to clean five houses. They each have their lunches packed, their knee pads in hand and hair pulled up. Mya's hair like a cinnamon bun. Neri wears a ponytail so she can spin it when she's bored. Every morning, they trade spots as leader to give out cleaning assignments. Today, Yvonne gives the orders. They split the cleaning depending on the size of the house and number of rooms. This house is two stories with four bedrooms and three bathrooms. It is Neri's turn to clean the bathrooms and Mya's turn to clean bedrooms. It always takes two to exorcise the filth from the kitchen. Yvonne volunteers and partners with Nayeli. Diana and Mya clean upstairs. Lupita and Neri clean downstairs. Neri puts her knee pads on and pep talks something like "everyone takes shits" in case a floater or a skid mark presents itself to her. With yellow gloves, science goggles, a sanitary face mask, a pink bucket and a utility belt with scrubbing devices, she knocks on the bathroom door and goes inside after moments of silence. The theme is ducks. Neri scribbles into a flip notepad and slides it into her utility belt. Ducks. Sea shells. Daisies. Boats. Affluence means affording an abundance of tacky and wonderful decorative flaws. Someone knocks on the door and Neri looks over her shoulder. There's a white boy with blue eyes. Maybe home for the summer. He excuses himself and asks Neri if he can step inside for private matters. She takes her face mask off and smiles. He reciprocates. Neri fans herself and steps away from the door so she can't hear the stream of pee from the duck bathroom. The young man comes out and tells Neri that he likes her curly hair. Neri blushes so she quickly puts her face mask back on and echoes a thank you.

Mya carries the vacuum in one arm and rose scented carpet powder in the other. She knocks on the door and goes into a room with posters of pretty women and angry looking men in all black clothing, two guitars on the ground, a drum set and a giant entertainment center. Mya plugs in the vacuum and aligns the strokes of the suction into perfect straight lines. She hums underneath the bustle of the vacuum. She takes two steps back and two steps forward. She moves her hips in figure eights. She dances alone and laughs. She thinks about the moments when she danced close to strangers at night clubs and then never saw them again. Mya continues to dance and stumbles over the cord. Her body shifts and she takes the vacuum down with her. The TV clicks off. A young guero walks in and runs toward the unplugged chord. Mya grabs her left hip. She picks herself up and looks at the boy. She waves her hands and says sorry, so sorry. His face is red and he tells her to get the fuck out. Before she can get to the outlet, he pulls the vacuum chord out and throws the rose powder out of the room. His lips are pursed as he pushes the vacuum. Get out. Get out. Get out. He says it three times as if he were counting down. Mya plugs the vacuum in and clears up his spill then heads to the rest of her assigned rooms to finish cleaning in time.

In the van, Mya says nothing. Neri grabs her bun and tells Mya she looks lovely when she's angry. You look like a nurturer. Mya pulls away. Mya tells the women: in my past life, I was a messenger dove. A veiled woman, perhaps a bruja, whispered mensajes to me every morning. Todos los días, a scroll manifested itself in my nest for me to deliver. I delivered them to gente in front of la Iglesia de San Andrés Xecul. I transported the scrolls to locals, tourists, abuelas, and children. The veiled woman whispered to me about lineage and solitude. Every morning, I heard the same message and every morning, I gave a scroll to someone new. I did this for years and years until one afternoon, I tried to fly home and a plastic bag caught me in mid-air. I fell to the ground and slid on the gravel at the mercy of the gusty winds. I slid and I slid until I woke up in this body.

When the van stops in front of the office, las mujeres get out and Neri hugs Mya. She takes Mya to a rose garden in Mariposa Park. Neri lets her hair down and tells Mya: when I was six or seven, I thought eating flower petals could turn me into a flower. I picked flower petals and ate them until all I could do was burp up perfume and dream about floral infestations taking over my intestines. She picks petals off of a pink rose and places them on her tongue. She picks more and more and chews them up and sticks her tongue out at Mya. Is it working? Mya shakes her head. It will work eventually.

SWEET GUM

It snowed the night you told me we should separate. I went outside with no shoes and no coat. I cried as frost collected on the cars and in my hair. We met four summers back. Four years was nothing. That's what my older friends used to say. I wanted to crawl back into bed with you. The urge to say sorry was overwhelming even if I wasn't sure what to be sorry for. I went back into the apartment and you sat in silence. I said nothing. You said nothing. It went on for days in between my bursts of crying which I couldn't help. I had to stay with you for a month until I could find a place of my own. Anytime you left the apartment, I called you and called you and you never answered. I knew you were with other women. I knew, but it wasn't anything I could stop. It wasn't my place. I found a small house with cheap rent and I painted it purple. I used neon pieces of construction paper as wallpaper and napped every single day for three months.

The first night I decided to go out it was because I stepped on a flyer to a three-story night club, "Area

21" on my way home. The flyer promised free drinks before 10 and an art gallery tucked away in a tent on the roof of the building. At the entrance, the bouncer stifled laughter when he saw me. He pointed at my mid-section and told me if I cut my black tee shirt into a crop top, I could go in. I scratched my scalp and slid lipstick on my mouth. He handed me the scissors. I took my shirt off and cut above the belly button. I put my shirt back on went around him as he caught drift of fake IDs. Heard him tell the girls they could go in if one of them cut slits into the side of her dress. I nudged at the short purple door and crawled through the entryway. I crawled inside a black and white checkered tunnel that led my body up and down until I tasted artificial fog and saw pulsating white light.

Area 21 is an old office building with sticky floors and vomit phantoms. Cubicles from the previous 9-5 ghosts are individually themed. I picked "Mermaid Cavern" because a young pretty couple took "Manatee Mansion." I danced alone as lasers splattered sweaty messes meshing together. I bumped into a masked man and woman. One of them offered me a drink. I declined. The woman offered me shrooms and I stuffed the fungus into my bra. The masked people attempted conversations. I covered their mouths and shook my head. We danced close. I tasted their exhaling breaths. They tasted my fingers. I left them in the Manatee Mansion and headed toward the center of the club. I chugged water from the mouth of a spitting angel water fountain and then followed an exit sign home.

* * *

Sweat is clinging onto clumpy strings of curls and down my temples. I had a dream about a neighborhood burning. My house was engulfed in emerald flames. Smoke twirled around me. I grabbed at my throat and coughed out silence. I woke up alone. The piercing through my gut is thick. I can hear the branch digging into the mattress underneath me. The sweet gum's branches are growing fast. I can't wipe away the dark arms of the tree reaching toward me like I usually do to the shadow people of sleep paralysis. The sweet gum grazes my cheek. A twig initially tickles. Then, with all its might, it settles into my bicep. The thought to scream is secondary to the creeping regret of never having a child. I regret not leaving with the masked couple. I regret not erasing you completely out of my memory.

I imagined you as the father to my kid because of your persistence on calling yourself a future soccer dad. I drove to Arizona in the summer. I hiked down the Grand Canyon alone, tasting dust and wishing you could see how much it looks like a painting. Our little girl, vocal and stubborn, a combo of you and I would say that it looked better in HD. If I had given birth, my endurance for this pain could compare. I could claim this was nothing because I brought a god damned human being onto this floating speck in space. She would be my gift to you along with a box full of this sweet gum's spiked capsules.

I am stuck to these branches and twigs soaking my mattress with reds of Blood Type O. I only figured this out because you told me what yours was at a house party as meaningless mingling and curiosity brewed for my own. This is where we first met. You called me pretty. You told me you enjoyed the cadence of my laughter. I shook your hand and waved as I left the party.

The sweet gum continues to expand and reach into my home. Parts of the ceiling are crumbling into a skylight. Patches of twinkling atmosphere expose themselves. The air is cold and still. Every breath is harsh. I can still smell hints of the earth.

I couldn't hear the message you left me on New Year's Eve because I had just kissed someone new and music was blurring into drunken ears. I danced against a person I didn't care for and I felt his warmth at the end of the night. I deleted your number, but I had it memorized. I never read the long texts you sent me because I was finally sincere with my disdain. I missed your last voicemail because I was busy at work. You got stuck on the interstate driving from Illinois. Tornado sirens wailed at plots of people piled into cars. You said you loved me and apologized about some bullshit we argued over before you bolted to a woman you met online. I was adamant on not speaking to you, so I erased the message and called you a fucking liar under my breath.

I went to the movies alone. It was a B-movie about wizards. I wore 3D glasses inside and reached toward the screen when the leading wizard winked at the audience. She stepped out of the screen and sat next to me. She showed me her pet scorpion and the constellations on its tail. She didn't need a wand, she simply needed her hands to cast spells. She took her hands and gently placed my hair behind my ears. She waved her hands from side to side and LED lights dispersed from the ceiling. They synchronized in colors then they blinked at different rhythms and colors. She snapped her fingers and mirrors surrounded the audience. We sat amongst makeshift stars with our buckets of popcorn and crinkly wrappers collecting on the ground. I walked out of the theater and I wanted to call you. The movie ends with the head wizard winking and blowing a kiss as she makes the theater pitch black. Droplets from the ceiling landed on my head and exposed skin. I felt hundreds of legs crawling on me. I sat in darkness and applauded. The lights came on and my skin was covered in pink and purple dust. The crawling came from the scorpions let loose as a consolation prize for watching the movie. I thought you might like the ending. I left you a message and asked you to call me back.

Sirens go in and out of my hearing and a helicopter's searchlight seeps through the cracks of this foundation. Gray is filling up my sight. I can't feel the branches or the cold air. I catch glimpses of an overcast beach, holding your hand, running up and down the shore, finding an abandoned bouquet that you said Poseidon delivered to me because of how much potential I had at nineteen.

LA REINA

The crown of nopales reaches up at the stars with pink and yellow flowers hidden due to the darkness, but unafraid to blossom when Reina wakes in the morning to watch over the children. She paints her face with blue, red, yellow and white. Small triangles in blue on each cheek and lines from ear to ear, gliding over the bridge of her nose like a heart monitor pulse mimicking mountain ranges on the earth below. The children line up in the morning to get a glimpse of Reina. She sits on a throne made of crystals in her deep violet gown with rainbows of geometric patterns following the seams. She wears earrings made of black scorpions and a ring on each finger representing the stars she's had the pleasure of visiting. She smiles at them always. She notices the ones who are becoming more and more transparent each morning. They are becoming part of the nebulous disorganization in the cosmos. They are becoming bigger than themselves. Her chest is heavy every day as she loses them, one by one. So, she goes to earth every night. She travels down the black spiral staircase stretching from the sky to the earth to float around and look through the windows of homes about to lose the child inside. Her feet are silent down the steps. She sniffs out abnormally slow hearts and looks inside window panes. She can see blue lips glowing and parents dreaming. She can see the little soul stretching and yawning. Reina motions at the child. Looking into his eyes, she can see his chronological health complications and DNA strands shrinking and snapping. Reina smiles at the child. Her smile is brighter than the full moon and the child walks toward her. She carries him up the spiral staircase in silence and shows him the cloud garden. The clouds sprout springs of white. Some of the vines reach higher than the child can see. Reina tells him not to be afraid. She tells him to play until the day he is finally gone.

Reina is not the only being looking for souls. There are fouler creatures and more nurturing ones too. Reina leaves the children be. She leaves them to their imaginations. The bear cub lures children with her cuteness. She lets the children pet her and then leads them to the shadow forest. Those souls become echoes. Background noise. The souls become those moments when you hear your name in silence and there's no one there. El alacran carries souls on his back into caverns where the souls become stalactites and stalagmites. Cave pools soak up the remnants of the ones who couldn't choose between being stuck in the sky or rooted to the earth. La llorona drowns the souls and wails as they are in the grasp of her arms. These souls become the grit in your throat that you gain before crying. Reina cannot save them all, but she saves the ones she can. The trace she leaves behind on this planet is in one patch of the Sahara desert. If you find the patch and place the sand under a microscope, you can see miniature skeletons in the fetal position, as though they fell asleep inside tiny capsules.

MARIGOLDS

"The spirit of our Tía Lily sits in the swing set we bought from the garage sale the other week. She is like a Llorona wannabe. She wails at night, except it's for you."

This is what my brother Jesus tells me. Why is he saying this as I am about to fall asleep?

"Mira, estupido, quiero dormir en paz."

He brings me a candle of La Virgen and tells me to light it for Tía.

"Tell her how you're doing in school. I think she will appreciate it."

I think he misses Tía Lily. She taught him how to read in Spanish and English. She also taught him the phrase "Shut the front door". He yells it to shock people. I haven't found the thrill in yelling obscenities or mimicking them. I called a girl a pendeja once and got detention for a week. I had to make a list of why she wasn't a pendeja even though that was a lie. She took my lunch money on several occasions. Jesus told me to defend myself. On the way home he asked me to punch him in the face. Little fists bundled together. I tried. I cried instead.

"I am weak, Jesus. I can't say no to her because I have a tender head. If she pulls my hair, I will fall to the ground and the spirit of Selena will be my only saving grace, me entiendes?"

Jesus hugged me and told me stories about Tía Lily. Tía Lily was sick and she managed to laugh and be mean to people every day, even when pendejos told her she should be sad about dying soon, but grateful to still be alive. Tía Lily went to the house of an ex and threw a big gulp of Fanta at his face and claimed it was holy water for his crooked soul. She ate tres leches every single day and told me to never trust a man if my gut told me not to.

I miss her too. Snot trails down my lips and onto my wrist. I grab the Vicks just in case anyone sees me cry. I can explain that I am acting and show them the Vicks on my face como en esa película where the girl lied in court. I light my candle and put it on my window sill. Jesus is in his sleeping bag next to me.

"Jesus? Do you want to play outside?"

"Esmai, it's late. Plus, Tía Lily is out there. I'm telling the truth."

"Then, let's talk to her. I can't fall asleep until I know you're not lying to me."

"Fine. Entonces, bring your candle and grab your favorite toy."

"Why?"

"We are going to bury it and have a memorial for Tía Lily."

"¿Y tú? Are you bringing something too?"

He digs into his sleeping bag and brings out a red Power Ranger action figure. I grab my yellow Power Ranger action figure and put on my yellow ranger mask. They sold out of all the pink ones and mamá could only afford one costume at a time. Jesus got to be the red ranger like he wanted. He told me the yellow ranger had superb fighting skills in comparison to the pink one. It's April now, but I can feel my strength increase after I put on the mask so I wear it often. Jesus finds a plastic purple shovel from our trip to Cali last summer. I follow behind him in my mask with the candle in one hand and the yellow ranger in the other.

"We need flowers for Tía Lily."

Our fence has honeysuckle hanging off of it. I stick my mask on top of my head. I pluck the sticky petals and inhale them after I have a pile in my palms. Jesus is digging a mini-grave for his power ranger. He hands me the shovel. I kiss the yellow ranger on the forehead and tell her to say hi to my Tía. I dig until I am sure the yellow ranger will fit into the grave. I place her in and slowly sprinkle dirt on her. I take my leg and shove the remaining dirt over her. I spread the honeysuckle petals over the two graves and place the candle in between them. Jesus holds my hand and we bow our heads.

I accidentally fall asleep with my yellow ranger mask on and I wake up to a bunch of indents in my face. Mamá is watching celebrity gossip and Jesus runs toward me with his mouth wide open.

"Jesus, your breath stinks."

"Shut up, Esmai. Come outside with me."

He grabs my wrist and I stomp out in pajamas and messy hair.

"Tía Lily?"

Marigolds are scattered in the backyard. I step into the yard and the pile is up to my knees. Did she leave these behind as a reminder to honor her in November? Mamá could not say no with a sign like this. Anytime we visited the cemetery, we prayed quickly and left with haste. Mamá told us she didn't want a bad spirit following us home so we always listened.

Jesus is rolling in the marigolds. I grab a handful and stick them in my sleeping bag. I run back outside.

"Jesus, is this Tía Lily sending us a sign?"

"I think so."

"What do you think it means?"

"No se, Esmai. I'm only a kid."

I don't know what it means either. I sit with my legs crossed and look at the sun settled alone in the sky. The purple spots emerge and I look over at Jesus. I exist in a space with good souls. I exist in this space and it inevitably ends.

ABOUT THE AUTHOR:

Rios de la Luz was born in Los Angeles, raised in El Paso, Texas and Oklahoma. She is an editor at *redfez. net* and runs *Ladyblog,* an extension of Ladybox Books. Her story, "Ear to the Ground," was featured on *Vol. 1 Brooklyn*. She is currently living in Portland, OR with her beautiful beast dog and her planetary partner. This is her first collection.

ACKNOWLEDGMENTS

Special thanks to mi amor (JDO), Constance, Mari, Ally, Liana, Michelle, Olivia, Valeria, Therkelson, Carly, Laura, Jesse, Erin, Mallory, Pearl, Sandra, Jack, Natasha, Anna, Kale, Monica, Jenna, Amina, Alicia, Rai, Cassandra, Laili, Naifeh, Kirsten Alene, Tiffany Scandal, Gabino Iglesias, Michael Kazepis, Marybeth McCauley, Grant Wamack, Monica Drake, Cameron Pierce, Chris Lambert, Brian Allen Carr, Matthew Revert, Chris Conklin, Troy James Weaver, Juliet Escoria, Selena (La Reina), Mister Spock and the most wonderful beast on the planet, Sleazimo.

AVAILABLE FROM BROKEN RIVER BOOKS

Death Don't Have No Mercy by William Boyle
On the Black by Ed Dinger
Scores by Robert Paul Moreira
The Blind Alley by Jake Hinkson
Will the Sun Ever Come Out Again? by Nate Southard
Visions by Troy James Weaver
The Principle by J David Osborne
Our Love Will Go The Way Of The Salmon by Cameron Pierce
The Last Projector by David James Keaton
Jungle Horses by Scott Adlerberg
Leprechaun in the Hood: The Musical: A Novel by Cameron
Pierce, Adam Cesare, and Shane McKenzie
Long Lost Dog Of It by Michael Kazepis
The Fix by Steve Lowe
Repo Shark by Cody Goodfellow
Incarnations by Chris Deal
Our Blood In Its Blind Circuit by J David Osborne
The First One You Expect by Adam Cesare
XXX Shamus by Red Hammond
Gravesend by William Boyle
Street Raised by Pearce Hansen
Peckerwood by Jedidiah Ayres
The Least of My Scars by Stephen Graham Jones

AVAILABLE FROM LADYBOX BOOKS

Jigsaw Youth by Tiffany Scandal

AVAILABLE FROM KING SHOT PRESS

Leverage by Eric Nelson
Strategies Against Nature by Cody Goodfellow
Killer &Victim by Chris Lambert

Made in the USA
Columbia, SC
20 November 2024

46722749R00074